CONTENTS

NOTE TO THE READER

The Godfather is a well-known book by Mario Puzo. It became a very popular movie. While it is not a true story, many people feel it offers a realistic view into the world of organized crime.

Every writer has a special voice. That is why we call our series *Writers' Voices*. We chose *The Godfather* because Mario Puzo's voice can be clearly heard as he dramatically portrays a world few of us know. In choosing a part from the book, we looked for an episode that would show the motivations and values of the characters in the book.

Reading "About the Selection from *The Godfather*" on page 11 will help you begin thinking about what you will read in the selection.

In addition to a selection from *The Godfather,* this book includes chapters with interesting and helpful information related to the selection. You may read these before or after reading the selection. You may choose to read some or all of these chapters.

- If you would like more information about what motivated Mario Puzo to write *The Godfather*, look at the chapter "Selected from *The Godfather Papers*" on page 51.

- Many readers enjoy finding out about the person who wrote the selection. Sometimes this information will give you more insight into the selection. You can find out more about Mario Puzo in the chapter on page 58.

If you are a new reader, you may want to have this book read aloud to you, perhaps more than once. Even if you are a more experienced reader, you may enjoy hearing it read aloud before reading it silently to yourself.

We encourage you to read *actively*. Here are some things you can do:

BEFORE READING

- Read the front and back covers of the book, and look at the cover illustration. Ask yourself what you expect the book to be about.

- Think about why you want to read this book. Perhaps you enjoyed seeing the movie *The Godfather*.
- Look at the Contents page. See where you can find a map showing where the story takes place and other information. Decide what you want to read and in what order.

DURING READING

- There may be Italian words or other words that are difficult to read. Keep reading to see if the meaning becomes clear. If it doesn't, go back and reread the difficult part or discuss it with others. Or look in the glossary on page 63 to see if you can find the word and its definition. Or look up the words in the dictionary.
- Ask yourself questions as you read. For example: How do powerful people get what they want?

AFTER READING

- Think about what you have read. Did you identify with Johnny Fontane? Or did the selection change your thinking about organized crime?

• Talk with others about your thoughts.

• Try some of the questions and activities in "Questions for the Reader" on page 45. They are meant to help you discover more about what you have read and how it relates to you.

The editors of *Writers' Voices* hope you will write to us. We want to know your thoughts about our books.

THE GODFATHER

The Godfather is a realistic and exciting story of the powerful Mafia "families" in the United States. Each family is made up of people who owe allegiance to a Don, the head of the family. The novel shows how these families hold power through the use of force and fear.

Mario Puzo didn't know about the Mafia from his own experience when he wrote the book. He has said, "I never met a real honest-to-god gangster." He researched the information he needed for his story.

Puzo's main character is the Sicilian-American Don Vito Corleone, head of the Corleone family. He is known, with great respect, as "the Godfather."

In the book, Puzo tells us this: "Don Vito Corleone was a man to whom everybody came for help, and never were they disappointed. He made no empty promises, nor the craven excuse that his hands were tied by more powerful forces in the world than himself. It was not necessary that he be your friend, it was not even important that you had no means with which to repay him. Only one thing was required. That you, *you yourself,* proclaim your friendship. And then, no matter how poor or powerless the supplicant, Don Corleone would take that man's troubles to his heart. And he would let nothing stand in the way to a solution of that man's woe. His reward? . . . It was understood, it was mere good manners, to proclaim that you were in his debt and that he had the right to call upon you at any time to redeem your debt by some small service."

The selection from *The Godfather* begins on a Saturday in August 1945. People are gathered at Don Corleone's home on Long Island for his daughter's marriage. After the wedding, while the party goes on, the Don retires to the corner room that is his office. Here he will receive, one by one, those who seek the favors of a man of his power.

Johnny Fontane has come to the wedding from California. He is a famous singer but his career is fading. A movie is about to be made which has a part that would make Johnny a star. But the head of the movie studio, Jack Woltz, refuses to give Johnny the part.

Johnny has come to ask for Don Corleone's help with his career. But Johnny believes that Jack Woltz is too powerful for even the Godfather to influence. During the Second World War, recently ended, Woltz performed many services for the government. He is an advisor to the president of the United States and a friend of J. Edgar Hoover, the powerful director of the Federal Bureau of Investigation (FBI).

But Don Corleone promises Johnny that he will get the part in Woltz's movie. Tom Hagen will carry out the Don's wishes. Hagen, an orphan who grew up in Don Corleone's home, is the family lawyer. He has just become the Don's *Consigliori,* a position of great trust and privilege.

Perhaps the selection will make you think about how some powerful people get what they want.

MAPS OF PLACES MENTIONED
IN THE SELECTION

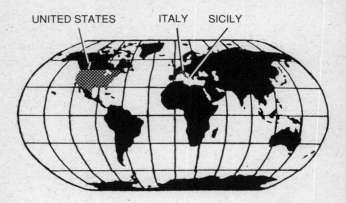

THE GODFATHER

Mario Puzo

"Now I want you to follow my orders," the Don said. "I want you to stay in my house for one month. I want you to eat well, to rest and sleep. I want you to be my companion, I enjoy your company, and maybe you can learn something about the world from your Godfather that might even help you in the great Hollywood. But no singing, no drinking and no women. At the end of the month you can go back to Hollywood and this *pezzonovante*, this .90 caliber will give you that job you want. Done?"

Johnny Fontane could not altogether believe that the Don had such power. But his Godfather had never said such and such a thing could be done without having it done. "This guy is a personal friend of J. Edgar Hoover," Johnny said. "You can't even raise your voice to him."

"He's a businessman," the Don said blandly. "I'll make him an offer he can't refuse."

"It's too late," Johnny said. "All the contracts have been signed and they start shooting in a week. It's absolutely impossible."

Don Corleone said, "Go, go back to the party. Your friends are waiting for you. Leave everything to me."

It was late Sunday night before Tom Hagen could kiss his wife good-bye and drive out to the airport. With his special number one priority (a grateful gift from a Pentagon staff general officer) he had no trouble getting on a plane to Los Angeles.

It had been a busy but satisfying day for Tom Hagen. Genco Abbandando had died at three in the morning and when Don Corleone returned from the hospital, he had informed Hagen that he was now officially the new *Consigliori* to the family. This meant that Hagen was sure to become a very rich man, to say nothing of power.

The Don had broken a long-standing tradition. The *Consigliori* was always a full-blooded Sicilian, and the fact that Hagen had been brought up as a member of the Don's family made no difference to that tradition. It was a question of blood. Only a Sicilian born to the ways of *omerta,* the law of silence, could be trusted in the key post of *Consigliori.*

Between the head of the family, Don Corleone, who dictated policy, and the operating level of men who actually carried out the orders of the Don, there were three layers, or buffers. In that way nothing could be traced to the top. Unless the *Consigliori* turned traitor. Each link of the chain would have to turn traitor for the Don to be involved and though it had never yet happened, there was always the possibility. The cure for that possibility also was known. Only one link in the chain had to disappear.

The *Consigliori* was also what his name implied. He was the counselor to the Don, his right-hand man, his auxiliary brain. He was also his closest companion and his closest friend. On important trips he would drive the Don's car, at conferences he would go out and get the Don refreshments, coffee and sandwiches, fresh cigars. He would know everything the Don knew or nearly everything, all the cells of power. He was the one man in the world who could bring the

Don crashing down to destruction. But no *Consigliori* had ever betrayed a Don, not in the memory of any of the powerful Sicilian families who had established themselves in America. There was no future in it. And every *Consigliori* knew that if he kept the faith, he would become rich, wield power and win respect. If misfortune came, his wife and children would be sheltered and cared for as if he were alive or free. *If he kept the faith.*

In some matters the *Consigliori* had to act for his Don in a more open way and yet not involve his principal. Hagen was flying to California on just such a matter. He realized that his career as *Consigliori* would be seriously affected by the success or failure of this mission.

The piston plane shook Tom Hagen's already nervous insides and he ordered a martini from the hostess to quiet them. Both the Don and Johnny had briefed him on the character of the movie producer, Jack Woltz. From everything that Johnny said, Hagen knew he would never be able to persuade Woltz. But he also had no doubt whatsoever that the Don would keep his promise to Johnny. His own role was that of negotiator and contact.

*　　*　　*

It was still dark when the plane landed in Los Angeles. Hagen checked into his hotel, showered and shaved, and watched dawn come over the city. He ordered breakfast and newspapers to be sent up to his room and relaxed until it was time for his ten A.M. appointment with Jack Woltz. The appointment had been surprisingly easy to make.

The day before, Hagen had called the most powerful man in the movie labor unions, a man named Billy Goff. Acting on instructions from Don Corleone, Hagen had told Goff to arrange an appointment on the next day for Hagen to call on Jack Woltz, that he should hint to Woltz that if Hagen was not made happy by the results of the interview, there could be a labor strike at the movie studio. An hour later Hagen received a call from Goff. The appointment would be at ten A.M. Woltz had gotten the message about the possible labor strike but hadn't seemed too impressed, Goff said. He added, "If it really comes down to that, I gotta talk to the Don myself."

"If it comes to that he'll talk to you," Hagen said. By saying this he avoided making any promises. He was not surprised that Goff was so agreeable to the Don's wishes. The family empire, technically, did not extend beyond the New York area but Don Corleone had first become strong by helping labor leaders. Many of them still owed him debts of friendship.

But the ten A.M. appointment was a bad sign. It meant that he would be first on the appointment list, that he would not be invited to lunch. It meant that Woltz held him in small worth. Goff had not been threatening enough, probably because Woltz had him on his graft payroll. And sometimes the Don's success in keeping himself out of the limelight worked to the disadvantage of the family business, in that his name did not mean anything to outside circles.

His analysis proved correct. Woltz kept him waiting for a half hour past the appointed time. Hagen didn't mind. The reception room was very plush, very comfortable, and on a plum-colored couch opposite him sat the most beautiful child Hagen had ever seen. She was no more than eleven or twelve, dressed in a very expensive but simple way as a grown woman. She had incredibly golden hair, huge deep sea-blue eyes and a fresh raspberry-red mouth. She was guarded by a woman obviously her mother, who tried to stare Hagen down with a cold arrogance that made him want to punch her in the face. The angel child and the dragon mother, Hagen thought, returning the mother's cold stare.

Finally an exquisitely dressed but stout middle-aged woman came to lead him through a string of offices to the office-apartment of the movie producer. Hagen was impressed by the beauty of the offices and the people working in them. He smiled. They were all shrewdies, trying to get their foot in the movie door by taking office jobs, and most of them would work in these offices for the rest of their lives or until they accepted defeat and returned to their home towns.

Jack Woltz was a tall, powerfully built man with a heavy paunch almost concealed by his perfectly tailored suit. Hagen knew his history. At ten years of age Woltz had hustled empty beer kegs and pushcarts on the East Side. At twenty he helped his father sweat garment workers. At thirty he had left New York and moved West, invested in the nickelodeon and pioneered motion pictures. At forty-eight he had been the most powerful movie magnate in Hollywood, still rough-spoken, rapaciously amorous, a raging wolf ravaging helpless flocks of young starlets. At fifty he transformed himself. He took speech lessons, learned how to dress from an English valet and how to behave socially from an English butler. When his first wife died he married a world-famous and beautiful actress who didn't like acting. Now at the age of sixty he collected old master paintings, was a member of the President's Advisory Committee, and had set up a multimillion-dollar foundation in his name to promote art in motion pictures. His daughter had married an English lord, his son an Italian princess.

His latest passion, as reported dutifully by every movie columnist in America, was his own racing stables on which he had spent ten million dollars in the past year. He had made headlines by purchasing the famed English racing horse Khartoum for the incredible price of six hundred thousand dollars and then announcing that the undefeated racer would be retired and put to stud exclusively for the Woltz stables.

He received Hagen courteously, his beautifully, evenly tanned, meticulously barbered face contorted with a grimace meant to be a smile. Despite all the money spent, despite the ministrations of the most knowledgeable technicians, his age showed; the flesh of his face looked as if it had been seamed together. But there was an enormous vitality in his movements and he had what Don Corleone had, the air of a man who commanded absolutely the world in which he lived.

Hagen came directly to the point. That he was an emissary from a friend of Johnny Fontane. That this friend was a very powerful man who would pledge his gratitude and undying friendship to Mr. Woltz if Mr. Woltz would grant a small favor. The small favor would be the casting of Johnny Fontane in the new war movie the studio planned to start next week.

The seamed face was impassive, polite. "What favors can your friend do me?" Woltz asked. There was just a trace of condescension in his voice.

Hagen ignored the condescension. He explained. "You've got some labor trouble coming up. My friend can absolutely guarantee to make that trouble disappear. You have a top male star who makes a lot of money for your studio but he just graduated from marijuana to heroin. My friend will guarantee that your male star won't be able to get any more heroin. And if some other little things come up over the years a phone call to me can solve your problems."

Jack Woltz listened to this as if he were hearing the boasting of a child. Then he said harshly, his voice deliberately all East Side, "You trying to put muscle on me?"

Hagen said coolly, "Absolutely not. I've come to ask a service for a friend. I've tried to explain that you won't lose anything by it."

Almost as if he willed it, Woltz made his face a mask of anger. The mouth curled, his heavy brows, dyed black, contracted to form a thick line over his glinting eyes. He leaned over the desk toward Hagen. "All right, you smooth son of a bitch, let me lay it on the line for you and your boss, whoever he is. Johnny Fontane never gets that movie. I don't care how many guinea Mafia goombahs come out of the woodwork." He leaned back. "A word of advice to you, my friend. J. Edgar Hoover, I assume you've heard of him"—Woltz smiled sardonically—"is a personal friend of mine. If I let him know I'm being pressured, you guys will never know what hit you."

Hagen listened patiently. He had expected better from a man of Woltz's stature. Was it possible that a man who acted this stupidly could rise to the head of a company worth hundreds of millions? That was something to think about since the Don was looking for new things to put money into, and if the top brains of this industry were so dumb, movies might be the thing. The abuse itself bothered him not at all. Hagen had learned the art of negotiation from the Don himself. "Never get angry," the Don had instructed. "Never make a threat. Reason with people." The art of this was to ignore all insults, all threats; to turn the other cheek. Hagen had seen the Don sit at a negotiating table for eight hours, swallowing insults, trying to persuade a notorious and megalomaniac strong-arm man to mend his ways. At the end of the eight hours Don Corleone had thrown up his hands in a helpless gesture and said to the other men at the table, "But no one can reason with this fellow," and had stalked out of the meeting room. The strong-arm man had turned white with fear. Emissaries were sent to bring the Don back into the room. An agreement was reached but two months later the strong-arm man was shot to death in his favorite barbershop.

So Hagen started again, speaking in the most ordinary voice. "Look at my card," he said. "I'm a lawyer. Would I stick my neck out? Have I uttered one threatening word? Let me just say that I am prepared to meet any condition you name to get Johnny Fontane that movie. I think I've already offered a great deal for such a small favor. A favor that I understand it would be in your interest to grant. Johnny tells me that you admit he would be perfect for that part. And let me say that this favor would never be asked if that were not so. In fact, if you're worried about your investment, my client would finance the picture. But please let me make myself absolutely clear. We understand your no is no. Nobody can force you or is trying to. We know about your friendship with Mr. Hoover, I may add, and my boss respects you for it. He respects that relationship very much."

Woltz had been doodling with a huge, red-feathered pen. At the mention of money his interest was aroused and he stopped doodling. He said patronizingly, "This picture is budgeted at five million."

Hagen whistled softly to show that he was impressed. Then he said very casually, "My boss has a lot of friends who back his judgment."

For the first time Woltz seemed to take the

whole thing seriously. He studied Hagen's card. "I never heard of you," he said. "I know most of the big lawyers in New York, but just who the hell are you?"

"I have one of those dignified corporate practices," Hagen said dryly. "I just handle this one account." He rose. "I won't take up any more of your time." He held out his hand, Woltz shook it. Hagen took a few steps toward the door and turned to face Woltz again. "I understand you have to deal with a lot of people who try to seem more important than they are. In my case the reverse is true. Why don't you check me out with our mutual friend? If you reconsider, call me at my hotel." He paused. "This may be sacrilege to you, but my client can do things for you that even Mr. Hoover might find out of his range." He saw the movie producer's eyes narrowing. Woltz was finally getting the message. "By the way, I admire your pictures very much," Hagen said in the most fawning voice he could manage. "I hope you can keep up the good work. Our country needs it."

Late that afternoon Hagen received a call from the producer's secretary that a car would pick him up within the hour to take him out to Mr. Woltz's country home for dinner. She told him it would be about a three-hour drive but that the car was equipped with a bar and some hors d'oeuvres. Hagen knew that Woltz made the trip in his private plane and wondered why he hadn't been invited to make the trip by air. The secretary's voice was adding politely, "Mr. Woltz suggested you bring an overnight bag and he'll get you to the airport in the morning."

"I'll do that," Hagen said. That was another thing to wonder about. How did Woltz know he was taking the morning plane back to New York? He thought about it for a moment. The most likely explanation was that Woltz had set private detectives on his trail to get all possible information. Then Woltz certainly knew he represented the Don, which meant that he knew something about the Don, which in turn meant that he was now ready to take the whole matter seriously. Something might be done after all, Hagen thought. And maybe Woltz was smarter than he had appeared this morning.

The home of Jack Woltz looked like an implausible movie set. There was a plantation-type mansion, huge grounds girdled by a rich black-dirt bridle path, stables and pasture for a herd of horses. The hedges, flower beds and grasses were as carefully manicured as a movie star's nails.

Woltz greeted Hagen on a glass-panel air-conditioned porch. The producer was informally dressed in blue silk shirt open at the neck, mustard-colored slacks, soft leather sandals. Framed in all this color and rich fabric his seamed, tough face was startling. He handed Hagen an outsized martini glass and took one for himself from the prepared tray. He seemed more friendly than he had been earlier in the day. He put his arm over Hagen's shoulder and said, "We have a little time before dinner, let's go look at my horses." As they walked toward the stables he said, "I checked you out, Tom; you should have told me your boss is Corleone. I thought you were just some third-rate hustler Johnny was running in to bluff me. And I don't bluff. Not that I want to make enemies, I never believed in that. But let's just enjoy ourselves now. We can talk business after dinner."

Surprisingly Woltz proved to be a truly considerate host. He explained his new methods, innovations that he hoped would make his stable the most successful in America. The stables were all fireproofed, sanitized to the highest degree, and guarded by a special security detail of private detectives. Finally Woltz led him to a stall which had a huge bronze plaque attached to its outside wall. On the plaque was the name "Khartoum."

The horse inside the stall was, even to Hagen's inexperienced eyes, a beautiful animal. Khartoum's skin was jet black except for a diamond-shaped white patch on his huge forehead. The great brown eyes glinted like golden apples, the black skin over the taut body was silk. Woltz said with childish pride, "The greatest racehorse in the world. I bought him in England last year for six hundred grand. I bet even the Russian Czars never paid that much for a single horse. But I'm not going to race him, I'm going to put him to stud. I'm going to build the greatest racing stable this country has ever known." He stroked the horse's mane and called out softly, "Khartoum, Khartoum." There was real love in his voice and the animal responded. Woltz said to Hagen, "I'm a good horseman, you know, and the first time I ever rode I was fifty years old." He laughed. "Maybe one of my grandmothers in Russia got raped by a Cossack and I got his blood." He tickled

Khartoum's belly and said with sincere admiration, "Look at that cock on him. I should have such a cock."

They went back to the mansion to have dinner. It was served by three waiters under the command of a butler, the table linen and ware were all gold thread and silver, but Hagen found the food mediocre. Woltz obviously lived alone, and just as obviously was not a man who cared about food. Hagen waited until they had both lit up huge Havana cigars before he asked Woltz, "Does Johnny get it or not?"

"I can't," Woltz said. "I can't put Johnny into that picture even if I wanted to. The contracts are all signed for all the performers and the cameras roll next week. There's no way I can swing it."

Hagen said impatiently, "Mr. Woltz, the big advantage of dealing with a man at the top is that such an excuse is not valid. You can do anything you want to do." He puffed on his cigar. "Don't you believe my client can keep his promises?"

Woltz said dryly, "I believe that I'm going to have labor trouble. Goff called me up on that, the son of a bitch, and the way he talked to me you'd never guess I pay him a hundred grand a year under the table. And I believe you can get that fag he-man star of mine off heroin. But I don't care about that and I can finance my own pictures. Because I hate that bastard Fontane. Tell your boss this is one favor I can't give but that he should try me again on anything else. Anything at all."

Hagen thought, you sneaky bastard, then why the hell did you bring me all the way out here? The producer had something on his mind. Hagen said coldly, "I don't think you understand the situation. Mr. Corleone is Johnny Fontane's godfather. That is a very close, a very sacred religious relationship." Woltz bowed his head in respect at this reference to religion. Hagen went on. "Italians have a little joke, that the world is so hard a man must have two fathers to look after him, and that's why they have godfathers. Since Johnny's father died, Mr. Corleone feels his responsibility even more deeply. As for trying you again, Mr. Corleone is much too sensitive. He never asks a second favor where he has been refused the first."

Woltz shrugged. "I'm sorry. The answer is still no. But since you're here, what will it cost me to have that labor trouble cleared up? In cash. Right now."

That solved one puzzle for Hagen. Why Woltz was putting in so much time on him when he had already decided not to give Johnny the part. And that could not be changed at this meeting. Woltz felt secure; he was not afraid of the power of Don Corleone. And certainly Woltz with his national political connections, his acquaintanceship with the FBI chief, his huge personal fortune and his absolute power in the film industry, could not feel threatened by Don Corleone. To any intelligent man, even to Hagen, it seemed that Woltz had correctly assessed his position. He was impregnable to the Don if he was willing to take the losses the labor struggle would cost. There was only one thing wrong with the whole equation. Don Corleone had promised his godson he would get the part and Don Corleone had never, to Hagen's knowledge, broken his word in such matters.

Hagen said quietly, "You are deliberately misunderstanding me. You are trying to make me an accomplice to extortion. Mr. Corleone promises only to speak in your favor on this labor trouble as a matter of friendship in return for your speaking in behalf of his client. A friendly exchange of influence, nothing more. But I can see you don't take me seriously. Personally, I think that is a mistake."

Woltz, as if he had been waiting for such a moment, let himself get angry. "I understood perfectly," he said. "That's the Mafia style, isn't it? All olive oil and sweet talk when what you're really doing is making threats. So let me lay it on the line. Johnny Fontane will never get that part and he's perfect for it. It would make him a great star. But he never will be because I hate that pinko punk and I'm going to run him out of the movies. And I'll tell you why. He ruined one of my most valuable protégés. For five years I had this girl under training, singing, dancing, acting lessons, I spent hundreds of thousands of dollars. I was going to make her a star. I'll be even more frank, just to show you that I'm not a hard-hearted man, that it wasn't all dollars and cents. That girl was beautiful and she was the greatest piece of ass I've ever had and I've had them all over the world. She could suck you out like a water pump. Then Johnny comes along with that olive-oil voice and guinea charm and she runs off. She threw it all away just to make me ridiculous. A man in my position, Mr. Hagen, can't afford to look ridiculous. I have to pay Johnny off."

For the first time, Woltz succeeded in astounding Hagen. He found it inconceivable that a grown man of substance would let such trivialities affect his judgment in an affair of business, and one of such importance. In Hagen's world, the Corleones' world, the physical beauty, the sexual power of women, carried not the slightest weight in worldly matters. It was a private affair, except, of course, in matters of marriage and family disgrace. Hagen decided to make one last try.

"You are absolutely right, Mr. Woltz," Hagen said. "But are your grievances that major? I don't think you've understood how important this very small favor is to my client. Mr. Corleone held the infant Johnny in his arms when he was baptized. When Johnny's father died, Mr. Corleone assumed the duties of parenthood, indeed he is called 'Godfather' by many, many people who wish to show their respect and gratitude for the help he has given them. Mr. Corleone never lets his friends down."

Woltz stood up abruptly. "I've listened to about enough. Thugs don't give me orders, I give them orders. If I pick up this phone, you'll spend the night in jail. And if that Mafia goombah tries any rough stuff, he'll never know what hit him. Even if I have to use my influence at the White House."

The stupid, stupid son of a bitch. How the hell did he get to be a *pezzonovante*, Hagen wondered. Advisor to the President, head of the biggest movie studio in the world. Definitely the Don should get into the movie business. And the guy was taking his words at their sentimental face value. He was not getting the message.

"Thank you for the dinner and a pleasant evening," Hagen said. "Could you give me transportation to the airport? I don't think I'll spend the night." He smiled coldly at Woltz. "Mr. Corleone is a man who insists on hearing bad news at once."

While waiting in the floodlit colonnade of the mansion for his car, Hagen saw two women about to enter a long limousine already parked in the driveway. They were the beautiful twelve-year-old blond girl and her mother he had seen in Woltz's office that morning. But now the girl's exquisitely cut mouth seemed to have smeared into a thick, pink mass. Her sea-blue eyes were filmed over and when she walked down the steps toward the open car her long legs tottered like a crippled foal's. Her mother supported the child, helping her into the car, hissing commands into her ear. The mother's head turned for a quick furtive look at Hagen and he saw in her eyes a burning, hawklike triumph. Then she too disappeared into the limousine.

So that was why he hadn't got the plane ride from Los Angeles, Hagen thought. The girl and her mother had made the trip with the movie producer. That had given Woltz enough time to relax before dinner and do the job on the little kid. And Johnny wanted to live in this world? Good luck to him, and good luck to Woltz.

Tom Hagen went to his law office in the city on Thursday morning to catch up on his paper work.

The Don had not seemed surprised when Hagen returned from California late Tuesday evening and told him the results of the negotiations with Woltz. He had made Hagen go over every detail and grimaced with distaste when Hagen told about the beautiful little girl and her mother. He had murmured "*infamita,*" his strongest disapproval. He had asked Hagen one final question. "Does this man have real balls?"

Hagen considered exactly what the Don meant by this question. Over the years he had learned that the Don's values were so different from those of most people that his words also could have a different meaning. Did Woltz have character? Did he have a strong will? He most certainly did, but that was not what the Don was asking. Did the movie producer have the courage not to be bluffed? Did he have the willingness to suffer heavy financial loss delay on his movies would mean, the scandal of his big star exposed as a user of heroin? Again the answer was yes. But again this was not what the Don meant. Finally Hagen translated the question properly in his mind. Did Jack Woltz have the balls to risk everything, to run the chance of losing *all* on a matter of principle, on a matter of honor; for revenge?

Hagen smiled. He did it rarely but now he could not resist jesting with the Don. "You're asking if he is a Sicilian." The Don nodded his head pleasantly, acknowledging the flattering witticism and its truth. "No," Hagen said.

That had been all. The Don had pondered

the question until the next day. On Wednesday afternoon he had called Hagen to his home and given him his instructions. The instructions had consumed the rest of Hagen's working day and left him dazed with admiration. There was no question in his mind that the Don had solved the problem.

Hagen worked quickly and efficiently for the next three hours consolidating earning reports from the Don's real estate company, his olive oil importing business and his construction firm. None of them were doing well but with the war over they should all become rich producers. He had almost forgotten the Johnny Fontane problem when his secretary told him California was calling. He felt a little thrill of anticipation as he picked up the phone and said, "Hagen here."

The voice that came over the phone was unrecognizable with hate and passion. "You fucking bastard," Woltz screamed. "I'll have you all in jail for a hundred years. I'll spend every penny I have to get you. I'll get that Johnny Fontane's balls cut off, do you hear me, you guinea fuck?"

Hagen said kindly, "I'm German-Irish." There was a long pause and then a click of the phone being hung up. Hagen smiled. Not once had Woltz uttered a threat against Don Corleone himself. Genius had its rewards.

Jack Woltz always slept alone. He had a bed big enough for ten people and a bedroom large enough for a movie ballroom scene, but he had slept alone since the death of his first wife ten years before. This did not mean he no longer used women. He was physically a vigorous man despite his age, but he could be aroused now only by very young girls and had learned that a few hours in the evening were all the youth of his body and his patience could tolerate.

On this Thursday morning, for some reason, he awoke early. The light of dawn made his huge bedroom as misty as a foggy meadowland. Far down at the foot of his bed was a familiar shape and Woltz struggled up on his elbows to get a clearer look. It had the shape of a horse's head. Still groggy, Woltz reached and flicked on the night table lamp.

The shock of what he saw made him physically ill. It seemed as if a great sledgehammer had struck him on the chest, his heartbeat jumped erratically and he became nauseous. His vomit spluttered on the thick rug.

Severed from its body, the black silky head of the great horse Khartoum was stuck fast in a thick cake of blood. White, reedy tendons showed. Froth covered the muzzle and those apple-sized eyes that had glinted like gold were mottled the color of rotting fruit with dead, hemorrhaged blood. Woltz was struck by a purely animal terror and out of that terror he screamed for his servants and out of that terror he called Hagen to make his uncontrolled threats. His maniacal raving alarmed the butler, who called Woltz's personal physician and his second in command at the studio. But Woltz regained his senses before they arrived.

He had been profoundly shocked. What kind of man could destroy an animal worth six hundred thousand dollars? Without a word of warning. Without any negotiation to have the act, its order, countermanded. The ruthlessness, the sheer disregard for any values, implied a man who considered himself completely his own law, even his own God. And a man who backed up this kind of will with the power and cunning that held his own stable security force of no account. For by this time Woltz had learned that the horse's body had obviously been heavily drugged before someone leisurely hacked the huge triangular head off with an ax. The men on night duty claimed that they had heard nothing. To Woltz this seemed impossible. They could be made to talk. They had been bought off and they could be made to tell who had done the buying.

Woltz was not a stupid man, he was merely a supremely egotistical one. He had mistaken the power he wielded in his world to be more potent than the power of Don Corleone. He had merely needed some proof that this was not true. He understood this message. That despite all his wealth, despite all his contacts with the President of the United States, despite all his claims of friendship with the director of the FBI, an obscure importer of Italian olive oil would have him killed. Would actually have him killed! Because he wouldn't give Johnny Fontane a movie part he wanted. It was incredible. People didn't have any right to act that way. There couldn't be any kind of world if people acted that way. It was insane. It meant you couldn't do what you wanted with your own money, with the companies you owned, the power you had to give orders. It was ten times worse than communism. It had to be smashed. It must never be allowed.

Woltz let the doctor give him a very mild sedation. It helped him calm down again and to think sensibly. What really shocked him was the casualness with which this man Corleone had ordered the destruction of a world-famous horse worth six hundred thousand dollars. Six hundred thousand dollars! And that was just for openers. Woltz shuddered. He thought of this life he had built up. He was rich. He could have the most beautiful women in the world by crooking his finger and promising a contract. He was received by kings and queens. He lived a life as perfect as money and power could make it. It was crazy to risk all this because of a whim. Maybe he could get to Corleone. What was the legal penalty for killing a racehorse? He laughed wildly and his doctor and servants watched him with nervous anxiety. Another thought occurred to him. He would be the laughingstock of California merely because someone had contemptuously defied his power in such arrogant fashion. That decided him. That and the thought that maybe, maybe they wouldn't kill him. That they had something much more clever and painful in reserve.

Woltz gave the necessary orders. His personal confidential staff swung into action. The servants and the doctor were sworn to secrecy on pain of incurring the studio and Woltz's undying enmity. Word was given to the press that the racehorse Khartoum had died of an illness contracted during his shipment from England. Orders were given to bury the remains in a secret place on the estate.

Six hours later Johnny Fontane received a phone call from the executive producer of the film telling him to report for work the following Monday.

QUESTIONS FOR THE READER

THINKING ABOUT THE STORY

1. What was interesting for you about the selection from *The Godfather?*

2. Were there ways the events or people in the selection became important or special to you? Write about or discuss these.

3. What do you think were the most important things Mario Puzo wanted to say in the selection?

4. In what ways did the selection answer the questions you had before you began reading or listening?

5. Were any parts of the selection difficult to understand? If so, you may want to read or listen to them again. Discuss with your learning partners possible reasons why they were difficult.

THINKING ABOUT THE WRITING

1. How did Mario Puzo help you see, hear and
   feel what happened in the selection? Find the
   words, phrases or sentences that did this
   best.

2. Writers think carefully about their stories'
   settings, characters and events. In writing
   this selection, which of these things do you
   think Mario Puzo felt was most important?
   Find the parts of the story that support your
   opinion.

3. In the selection, Mario Puzo uses dialogue.
   Dialogue can make a story stronger and
   more alive. Pick out some dialogue that you
   feel is strong, and explain how it helps the
   story.

4. The selection from *The Godfather* is written
   from the point of view of someone outside
   the story who tells us what is happening.
   The writer uses the words "he" and "she" as
   opposed to "I" or "me." What difference
   does this create in the writing of the
   selection?

5. Mario Puzo, through his writing, makes us
   understand how a powerful person might
   think or act. Find some parts in the selection
   that helped you understand this.

ACTIVITIES

1. Were there any words that were difficult for you in the selection from *The Godfather?* Go back to these words and try to figure out their meanings. Discuss what you think each word means, and why you made that guess. Look them up in a dictionary and see if your definitions are the same or different.

   Discuss with your learning partners how you are going to remember each word. Some ways to remember words are to put them on file cards, write them in a journal, or create a personal dictionary. Be sure to use the words in your writing in a way that will help you to remember their meaning.

2. Talking with other people about what you have read can increase your understanding. Discussion can help you organize your thoughts, get new ideas and rethink your original ideas. Discuss your thoughts about the selection with someone else who has read it. Find out if you helped yourself understand the selection in the same or different ways. Find out if your opinions about the selection are the same or different. See if your thoughts change as result of this discussion.

3. After you finish reading or listening, you might want to write down your thoughts about the book. You could write your reflections on the book in a journal, or you could write about topics the book has brought up that you want to explore further. You could write a book review or a letter to a friend you think might be interested in the book.

4. Did reading the selection give you any ideas for your own writing? You might want to write about:
   • a powerful person you have known or heard about.
   • your thoughts about the right and wrong ways to use power.
   • your own values and how far you would go to defend them.

5. Mario Puzo made an outline of his story before he began writing *The Godfather*. You might try making an outline for a story you are planning to write.

6. If you could talk to Mario Puzo, what questions would you ask about his writing? You might want to write the questions in a journal.

THE GODFATHER PAPERS AND OTHER CONFESSIONS

In the book *The Godfather Papers*, Mario Puzo explains how he came to write *The Godfather*. He also tells of later working on the screenplay for the movie.

This selection is about the writing of the book, and of the great success that followed its publication in 1969.

Most books are first seen by publishers when they are completely written, but an author will sometimes offer only an outline of his idea (as was the case with *The Godfather*). The author's literary agent sends the book or outline to an editor at a publishing company. The publisher then decides if it wishes to publish the book.

If the publisher chooses to proceed, a contract is drawn up. This contract gives the publisher certain rights, among them:

- the right to publish the book in a hardcover edition.
- the right to give permission to a paperback publisher to publish the book, usually a year later, in a less expensive edition.

The contract also provides for the author to receive payments before the book has been published. These payments are called "advances" against royalties. A royalty is a percentage, the author's share of the price the publisher will charge for the book. The author's agent receives ten percent or more of what the author makes.

The paperback publisher also pays advances against royalties. These are paid to the hardcover publisher, who then shares them with the author.

Advances are risks for the publisher, since they are paid before any books are sold. The hardcover and the paperback publishers are gambling that their editions of the book will sell enough copies to justify the amount of money they have advanced.

The hardcover publisher of *The Godfather* was G. P. Putnam's Sons. Fawcett, the paperback publisher, paid a higher advance than had ever been paid before for the right to publish a book in paperback.

THE GODFATHER PAPERS AND OTHER CONFESSIONS
Mario Puzo

I have written three novels. *The Godfather* is not as good as the preceding two; I wrote it to make money. My first novel, *The Dark Arena* (1955), received mostly very good reviews saying I was a writer to watch. Naturally I thought I was going to be rich and famous. The book netted me $3,500.

My second novel, *The Fortunate Pilgrim*, was published ten years later (1965) and netted me $3,000. I was going downhill fast. Yet the book received some extraordinarily fine reviews.

Anyway I was a hero, I thought. But my publisher was not impressed. I asked for an advance to start on my next book and the editors were cool. They were courteous. They were kind. They showed me the door.

I couldn't believe it. I went back and read all the reviews on my first two books. (I skipped the bad ones.) There must be some mistake. I was acknowledged as a real talent at least.

Well, we had another talk. The editors didn't like the idea behind my new novel. One editor wistfully remarked that if *Fortunate Pilgrim* had only had a little more of that Mafia stuff in it maybe the book would have made money.

I was forty-five years old and tired of being an artist. Besides, I owed $20,000 to relatives, finance companies, banks and assorted bookmakers and shylocks. So I told my editors OK, I'll write a book about the Mafia, just give me some money to get started. They said no money until we see a hundred pages. I compromised, I wrote a ten-page outline. They showed me the door again.

There is no way to explain the terrible feeling of rejection, the damage, the depression and weakening of will such manipulation does to a writer. But this incident also enlightened me. I had been naïve enough to believe that publishers cared about art. They didn't. They wanted to make money.

I had never doubted I could write a best-selling commercial novel whenever I chose to do so. My writing friends, my family, my children and my creditors all assured me now was the time to put up or shut up.

I was willing, I had a ten-page outline—but nobody would take me. Months went by. But one day a writer friend dropped into my office. During lunch I told him some funny Mafia stories and [showed him] my ten-page outline. He was enthusiastic. He arranged a meeting for me with the editors of G. P. Putnam's Sons. The editors just sat around for an hour listening to my Mafia tales and said go ahead. They also gave me a $5,000 advance and I was on my way, just like that.

It took me three years to finish.

I'm ashamed to admit that I wrote *The Godfather* entirely from research. I never met a real honest-to-god gangster. I knew the gambling world pretty good, but that's all.

I finally had to finish *The Godfather* in July, 1968, because I needed the final $1,200 advance payment from Putnam to take my wife and kids to Europe. My wife had not seen her family for twenty years and I had promised her that this was the year. I had no money, but I had a great collection of credit cards. Still I needed that $1,200 in cash, so I handed in the rough manuscript. Before leaving for Europe, I told my publisher not to show the book to anybody; it had to be polished.

My family had a good time in Europe. When we finally got home, I owed the credit card companies $8,000.

I went into New York to see my agent, Candida Donadio. She informed me that my publisher had just turned down $375,000 for the paperback rights to *The Godfather*.

I had given strict orders it wasn't to be shown to even a paperback house, but this was no time to complain. I called my editor at Putnam, Bill Targ, and he said they were holding out for $410,000 because $400,000 was some sort of record. I hung around New York, had a very late lunch with Targ, and over our coffee he got a call. Ralph Daigh of Fawcett had bought the paperback rights for $410,000.

I decided to get home to Long Island. While waiting for my car, I called my brother to tell him the good news. This brother had 10 percent of *The Godfather* because he supported me all my life and gave me a final chunk of money to complete the book. Through the years I'd call him up frantic for a few hundred bucks to pay the mortgage or buy the kids shoes. He always came through. So now I wanted him to know that since my half of the paperback rights came to $205,000 (the hard-cover publisher keeps half), he was in for a little over twenty grand.

He is the kind of guy who is always home when I call to borrow money. Now that I had money to give back, he was naturally out. I got my mother on the phone. She speaks broken English but understands the language perfectly. I explained it to her.

She asked, "$40,000?"

I said no, it was $410,000. I told her three times before she finally answered, "Don't tell nobody." My car came out of the garage and I hung up. Traffic was jammed, and it took me over two hours to get home out in the suburbs. When I walked in the door, my wife was dozing over the TV and the kids were all out playing. I went over to my wife, kissed her on the cheek, and said, "Honey, we don't have to worry about money anymore. I just sold my book for $410,000."

She smiled at me and kept dozing.

When I got through with all the phone calls, my wife was in bed asleep. So were the kids. I went to bed and slept like a rock. When I woke up the next morning, my wife and kids circled the bed. My wife said, "What was that you said last night?" She had just grasped the whole thing.

Well, it's a nice happy ending. But nobody seemed to believe me. So I called Bill Targ and drew an advance check for $100,000. I paid my debts, paid my agents' commissions, paid my brother his well-deserved 10 percent and three months later I called my publishers and agent for more money. They were stunned. What about the huge check I had just gotten three months before. I couldn't resist. Why should I treat them any differently than I had treated my family all those lean years? "A hundred grand doesn't last forever," I said.

The Godfather to date had earned over $1,000,000, but I still wasn't rich. There were agents' commissions and lawyers' fees. There were federal and state income taxes. All of which cut the original million to less than half. But before I grasped all this I had a great time. I spent the money as fast as it came in. The only thing was that I felt very unnatural being out of debt. I didn't owe anybody one penny.

I loved the money, but I didn't really like being "famous." I found it quite simply distressing. I never much liked parties, never liked talking to more than two or three people at one time.

Anyway, to wind up. *The Godfather* became No. 1 best seller in the USA; sixty-seven weeks on *The New York Times* list; also No. 1 in England, France, Germany and other countries. It's been translated into seventeen or twenty languages, I stopped keeping track. They tell me it's the fastest and best-selling fiction paperback of all times or will be when the new "film edition" comes with the movie—but one can't believe everything publishers tell their authors.

The book got much better reviews than I expected. I wished like hell I'd written it better. I like the book. It has energy and I lucked out by creating a central character that was popularly accepted as genuinely mythic. But I wrote below my gifts in that book.

ABOUT MARIO PUZO

Mario Puzo was born to Italian immigrant parents in New York City on October 15, 1920. He grew up in a tenement in an area known as Hell's Kitchen, next to the New York Central Railroad yards.

Puzo's father worked for the railroad to support his wife, five sons and two daughters. But he deserted the family when Puzo was 12 years old.

Puzo's mother, Maria, was a strong woman. "I had every desire to go wrong but I never had a chance," Puzo says. "The Italian family structure was too formidable. I never came home to an empty house."

The Hudson Guild Settlement House, where Puzo played sports and hung out with his friends, was an important part of his early life. He calls it "a five-story field of joy for slum kids."

At the Guild, Puzo discovered books. He says, "At the age of sixteen when I let everybody know that I was going to be a great writer, my friends and family took the news quite calmly, my mother included. She did not become angry. She quite simply assumed that I had gone off my nut. She was illiterate, and her peasant life in Italy made her believe that only a son of the nobility could possibly be a writer."

To help support his family and himself, Puzo went to work for the railroad, thinking he might never escape the slums to achieve his dream of becoming a writer. But then World War II broke out, and he was sent to Germany by the U.S. Air Force. He returned home with a new wife, Erika, and their first child. He got a civil service job, but he also took classes in creative writing. He began writing stories.

Puzo's first story was published in 1950, his first book in 1955. In 1963, he quit his civil service job to work at a magazine and kept on writing stories and articles. *The Fortunate Pilgrim,* the book he is proudest of, was published in 1965. It is about Italian immigrants in New York City.

When Puzo was 45 years old, with five

children to support, he decided to write a book that would make a lot of money and free him to write full time.

The Godfather was published in 1969. It sold 9 million copies in two years, making it one of the most successful books in publishing history. And it went on to become a hit movie with two sequels.

Puzo calls himself an Italian success story. He lives and writes in Long Island, New York.

THE GODFATHER

Paramount Pictures bought the motion picture rights for *The Godfather* while Puzo was still writing the book. Later, after the book became a big bestseller, they hired Puzo to work on the screenplay.

Paramount hired Francis Ford Coppola to direct the film. Although he was only 31 years old and not well known as a director, Paramount felt he would do a good job, partly because he was Italian-American himself.

Coppola insisted that the movie be as real as possible. He said, "It was my intention to make this an authentic piece of film about gangsters who were Italian, how they lived, how they behaved, the way they treated their families, celebrated their rituals." Coppola worked with Puzo on writing the film.

The stars of the movie included Marlon Brando, Al Pacino, James Caan, Robert

Duvall and Diane Keaton. In 1972, *The Godfather* won Academy Awards for Best Picture and Best Screenplay. Marlon Brando won for Best Actor.

GLOSSARY

Consigliori. Counselor; in this story, the number-two person in a Mafia family who advises the Don and sees that his orders are carried out.

Cossack. A member of the Russian cavalry under the czars.

czars. The former rulers of Russia.

Don. A title of respect for the head of a Mafia family.

goombah. A comrade.

guinea. A derogatory word for an Italian.

infamità. Detestable or shameful.

Mafia. A secret organization involved in both lawful and unlawful activities.

omertà. The Sicilian law or oath of silence.

pezzonovante. Big shot.

protégé. Someone under the care and protection of an important person.

Seven series of good books for all readers:

WRITERS' VOICES
Selections from the works of America's finest and most popular writers, along with background information, maps, and other supplementary materials. Authors include: Kareem Abdul-Jabbar • Maya Angelou • Bill Cosby • Alex Haley • Stephen King • Loretta Lynn • Larry McMurtry • Amy Tan • Anne Tyler • Abigail Van Buren • Alice Walker • Tom Wolfe, and many others.

NEW WRITERS' VOICES
Anthologies and individual narratives by adult learners. A wide range of topics includes home and family, prison life, and meeting challenges. Many titles contain photographs or illustrations.

OURWORLD
Selections from the works of well-known science writers, along with related articles and illustrations. Authors include David Attenborough and Carl Sagan.

FOR YOUR INFORMATION
Clearly written and illustrated works on important self-help topics. Subjects include: Eating Right • Managing Stress • Getting Fit • About AIDS • Getting Good Health Care, among others.

TIMELESS TALES
Classic myths, legends, folk tales, and other stories from around the world, with special illustrations.

SPORTS
Fact-filled books on baseball, football, basketball, and boxing, with lots of action photos. With read-along tapes narrated by Phil Rizzuto, Frank Gifford, Dick Vitale, and Sean O'Grady.

SULLY GOMEZ MYSTERIES
Fast-paced detective series starring Sully Gomez and the streets of Los Angeles.

WRITE FOR OUR FREE COMPLETE CATALOG:

SIGNAL HILL

Signal Hill Publications
P.O. Box 131
Syracuse, NY 13210-0131